Life Without
Nico

ANDREA MATURANA

Life Without
Nico

FRANCISCO
JAVIER OLEA

Maia and Nico are best friends.
They never get bored of playing together.

Even when they aren't together,

it's as if they are.

But one day, Nico's father says they'll be moving far away for a while so he can continue his studies.

This news is hard to accept.

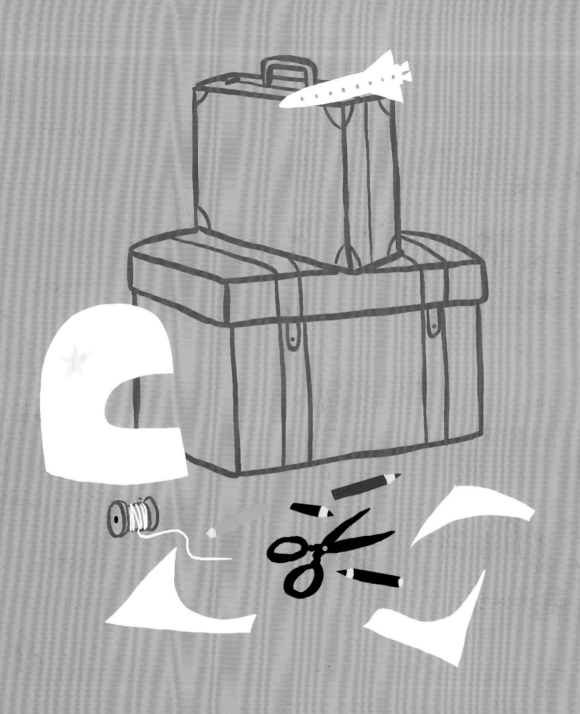

The days pass quickly.

Too soon, it's time to say goodbye.

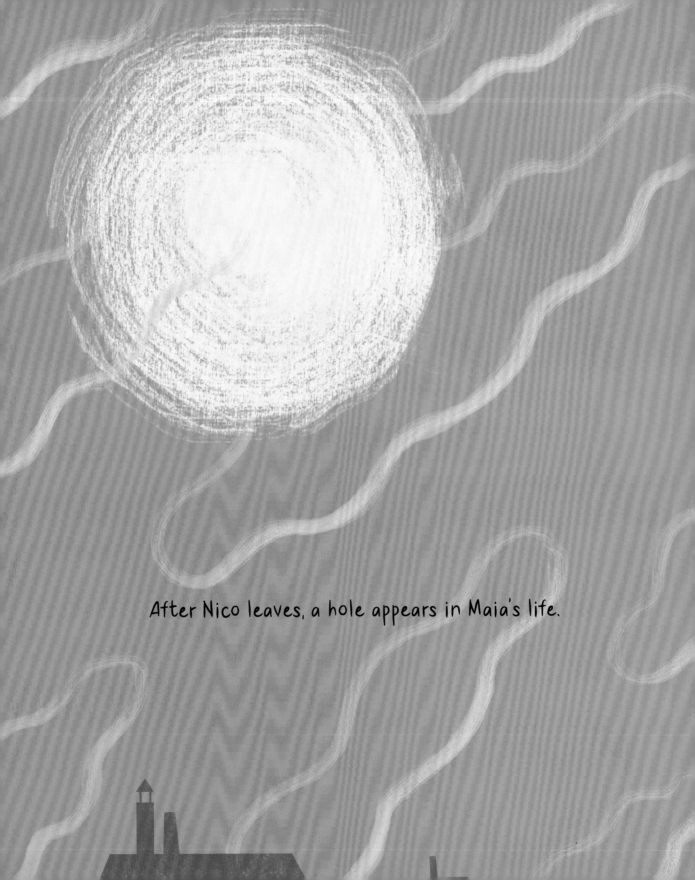

After Nico leaves, a hole appears in Maia's life.

The empty feeling grows ...

Now time passes slowly, and the emptiness follows Maia everywhere she goes.

It's boring. She can't play
with it, and it won't let
other children near.

Sometimes the days feel dark to Maia.
Other times everything feels far away.

But as time goes on, Maia meets
an unexpected companion ...

She makes a new friend ...

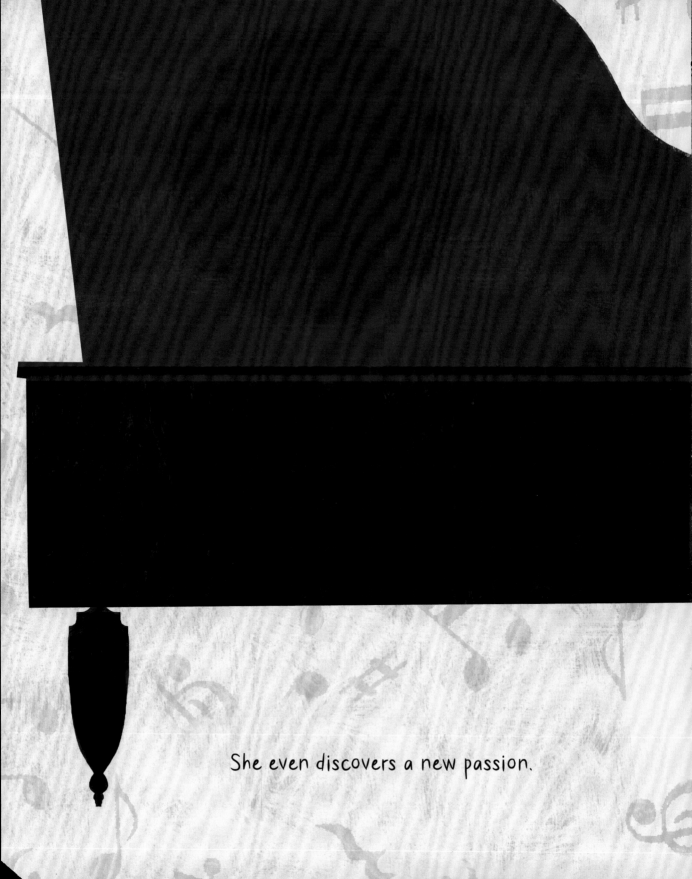

She even discovers a new passion.

When Maia talks to Nico, she tells him about
the kitten and her new friend. Nico describes
amazing animals, such as koalas and kangaroos.

And with the arrival of spring, everything begins to bloom.

Time starts running more
and more quickly, and Maia
stops counting the days.

Finally it's the day of
Nico's return.

Maia thought she would be happy,
but instead she's worried. Her life
has become so full. Will there be
enough room for Nico, too?

Then when Maia sees Nico, she understands.

There are some things time cannot change.

Originally published in Mexico under the title *La vida sin Santi* by Andrea Maturana and Francisco Javier Olea

© 2014 Fondo de Cultura Económica
Carretera Picacho Ajusco 227, C.P. 14738, México D.F.

English edition © 2016 Kids Can Press

Kids Can Press acknowledges the financial support of the Government of Ontario, through the Ontario Media Development Corporation's Ontario Book Initiative.

Published in Canada by
Kids Can Press Ltd.
25 Dockside Drive
Toronto, ON M5A 0B5

Published in the U.S. by
Kids Can Press Ltd.
2250 Military Road
Tonawanda, NY 14150

www.kidscanpress.com

The artwork in this book was rendered in Photoshop.
The text is set in Elisana.

Original edition edited by Marisol Ruiz Monter
English edition edited by Stacey Roderick
Designed by Miguel Venegas Geffroy

Manufactured in Shenzhen, China, in 9/2015 by C & C Offset

CM 16   0 9 8 7 6 5 4 3 2 1

LIBRARY AND ARCHIVES CANADA CATALOGUING IN PUBLICATION

Maturana, Andrea, 1969– [Vida sin Santi. English]
Life without Nico / written by Andrea Maturana ; illustrated by Francisco Javier Olea.

Translation of: La vida sin Santi.
ISBN 978-1-77138-611-1 (bound)

I. Olea, Francisco Javier, illustrator II. Title. III. Title: Vida sin Santi. English.

PZ7.M375Li 2016   j863'.64   C2015-904824-9

Kids Can Press is a CORUS™ Entertainment company

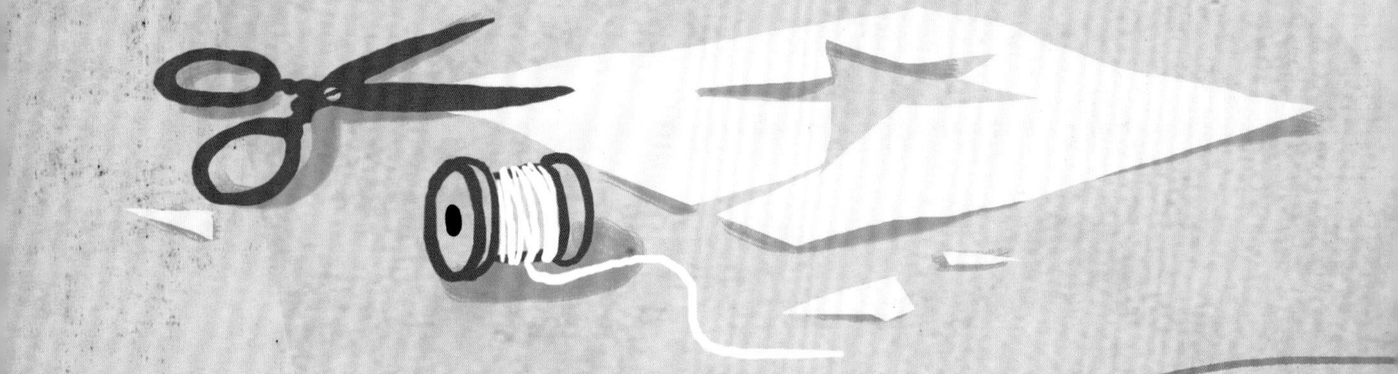